D0382339

Top 10 Sluggers

Chris W. Sehnert

ABDO & Daughters
Publishing

Published by Abdo & Daughters, 4940 Viking Drive, Suite 622, Edina, Minnesota 55435.

Copyright © 1997 by Abdo Consulting Group, Inc., Pentagon Tower, P.O. Box 36036, Minneapolis, Minnesota 55435 USA. International copyrights reserved in all countries. No part of this book may be reproduced in any form without written permission from the publisher.

Printed in the United States.

Cover and Interior Photo credits: Allsports Photos
                                  Wide World Photos
                                  Bettmann Photos
                                  Sports Illustrated

Edited by Paul Joseph

Library of Congress Cataloging-in-Publication Data

Sehnert, Chris W.
        Top 10 Sluggers / Chris W. Sehnert.
        p.   cm. -- (Top 10 Champions)
        Includes index.
        Summary: Covers the careers and statistics of ten notable baseball players, including Babe Ruth, Hank Aaron, and Roberto Clemente.
        ISBN 1-56239-797-4
        1. Baseball players--United States--Biography--Juvenile literature. 2. Batting (Baseball)--Juvenile literature. [1. Baseball players.] I. Title. II. Series: Sehnert, Chris W. Top 10 Champions.
        GV865.A.1S45   1997
        796.357'26'092273--dc21   97-14481
                                                                   CIP
                                                                   AC

Table of Contents

Babe Ruth

Baseball is a game for the ages. Its history as a professional sport began in 1869, but baseball's ancestry is older than the country that claims it as their national pastime. Out of all the great stars who have played the game, none have shone more brightly than Babe Ruth. The "Sultan of Swat" was Major League Baseball's finest left-handed pitcher early in his career. After being traded from the Boston Red Sox to the New York Yankees in 1920, he gave up his role as a hurler to set more than 50 major league batting records!

The "Bambino's" impact on baseball and the world was immediate and far-reaching, as were the long drives that flew off his mighty bat. Many of Babe's power-hitting standards are still pursued today, more than 60 years after his retirement. In the decade known as the "Roaring 20s," Babe's face was the most photographed image in the world. Much of the folklore surrounding his life sounds like fiction from a storybook. Some of it is, but Babe's ability to play baseball while enthralling the public, both on and off the field, was not a fantasy.

George Herman Ruth was born in Baltimore, Maryland. His parents were saloon keepers who had great difficulty controlling their son. He was classified as incorrigible at the age of seven and was shipped off to St. Mary's Industrial School for Boys. There, he came under the guidance of the school's disciplinarian, a giant of a man known as Brother Matthias. Abandoned by his family, George spent the rest of his childhood at the reform school where he was trained to be a shirt maker. Brother Matthias provided what turned out to be the most useful training, as George's father-figure and baseball coach.

Jack Dunn was the owner of Baltimore's minor league baseball team. When George Ruth turned 19 years old,

Dunn became his legal guardian and gave him a contract to pitch for his Orioles. Because of their legal relationship George soon became known as Dunn's "Babe." By mid-season with the Baltimore ballclub struggling financially, Dunn traded the Babe to the Boston Red Sox for cash. George's new nickname would follow him to the major leagues. Babe Ruth would soon become the most recognized name in all of baseball and the most celebrated *Champion* of the 20th Century!

During his six seasons with the Red Sox, Babe pitched for three World Championship teams, while setting a record for consecutive scoreless innings during the World Series. In various years, he led the American League (AL) in complete games, shutout victories, and earned run average (ERA), while compiling two 20 win seasons. Then in 1918, as a part-time outfielder the Babe led the league in home runs for the first time. His 11 long balls that season represented an average total for a home run champion. The "Dead Ball Era" was about to end. The next season, Babe set a single-season record crushing 29!

The deal that sent Babe Ruth to New York easily ranks as both the worst player-trade and greatest investment in the history of professional sports. The Yankees made the Bambino a full-time outfielder in his first season with the ballclub, and he responded by nearly redoubling his own previous single-season home run record. More than one-million fans attended New York's Polo Grounds for Yankee home games that season. There was little doubt what the record-setting crowds had come to see.

In 1935, Babe Ruth returned to Boston where he played the final games of his career as a member of the Braves. On May 25th of that season, the Babe connected three times to bring his career home run total to 714. One of those final swats cleared the rightfield roof of Pittsburgh's Forbes Field. He retired shortly thereafter. Babe Ruth was an entertainer of fantastic proportion and a baseball player for the ages.

PROFILE:
Babe Ruth
Born: February 6, 1895
Died: August 16, 1948
Height: 6' 2"
Weight: 215 pounds
Position: Outfield, First Base, and Pitcher
Teams: Boston Red Sox (1914-1919), New York Yankees (1920-1934), Boston Braves (1935)

CHAMPIONSHIP

SEASONS

1915
World Series
Boston Red Sox (4) vs.
Philadelphia Phillies (1)

1916
World Series
Boston Red Sox (4) vs.
Brooklyn Dodgers (1)

1918
World Series
Boston Red Sox (4) vs.
Chicago Cubs (2)

1923
World Series
New York Yankees (4) vs.
New York Giants (2)

1927
World Series
New York Yankees (4) vs.
Pittsburgh Pirates (0)

1928
World Series
New York Yankees (4) vs.
St. Louis Cardinals (0)

1932
World Series
New York Yankees (4) vs.
Chicago Cubs (0)

FACT OR FICTION

Babe Ruth was a true American Legend. Stories of his life are often assumed to be fairytales, when in fact most of them really happened. He truly was an oversized kid who snacked on hot dogs and soda pops by the dozen. He really did play ball with a group of children on a sandlot after a World Series game. He actually did break a window of a shop outside of St. Louis' Sportsmans Park with a long home run, one of many Ruthian blasts which literally left the yard!

Among the most disputed stories are those that entail Babe's ability to go deep on command. The facts are these. On the same day he delivered an autographed baseball to a bedridden boy in a hospital, Babe crushed three round-trippers each traveling further than the one before.

Babe Ruth

THE RUTH MYTH

In his final World Series, Babe faced the Chicago Cubs' pitcher Charlie Root in the fifth inning of Game 3. He had already launched a homer earlier in the game, but his defensive lapse in rightfield had allowed the Cubs to tie the score (4-4). With the crowd at Wrigley Field taunting his every move, Babe calmly held up one and then two fingers as Root slipped two pitches by him for strikes. Before sending the final pitch out of sight, Babe clearly pointed his bat in the direction of Root and the centerfield bleachers. Did he truly "Call his shot?" What do you believe?

Babe smashes a homer.

*T*HE HOUSE THAT RUTH BUILT

In 1923, New York's American League (AL) ballclub moved into Yankee Stadium and won their first World Championship. The new ballpark was immediately dubbed "the House that Ruth Built," and its so-called architect continued to hammer baseballs within through 12 more seasons!

Babe prepares to hit another pitch out of the park.

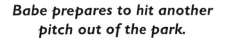

7

Joe DiMaggio

The New York Yankees have the greatest championship tradition in all of baseball. It stretches from the early 1920s, when Babe Ruth single-handedly ended the "Dead Ball Era," to the team's 23rd World Championship in 1996. In the season after Babe's retirement, a new face appeared in the "House that Ruth Built." He was a centerfielder with the swiftness of a "Yankee Clipper" sailing through the New York harbor. His handsome appearance appealed to Hollywood's most beautiful starlets, and his patriotism caused him to forego three seasons in order to serve his country in World War II. "Joltin' Joe" DiMaggio served the New York Yankees in all 13 of his major league seasons. During those years, he set an "unbreakable record" all his own, and led his team to nine World Championships!

Joseph Paul DiMaggio, Jr. was the fourth of five sons and eighth of nine children born to Joe, Sr. and Rosalia DiMaggio. His parents immigrated to the United States from Isola della Femmine, on the island of Sicily. Joe, Jr. was born in Martinez, California. He grew up in the Russian Hill district of San Francisco, where his father was a professional crab-fisherman. As a boy, Joe delivered newspapers and watched his older brothers dominate the baseball diamond.

The DiMaggio boys ruled San Francisco's sandlot scene for several seasons. While little Joe was leading his team to the championship of a local Boys Club League, his older brother Vince was playing centerfield for the minor-league San Francisco Seals. Brother Tom was said to be the most talented before following Joe, Sr.

into the fishing business. Vince, Joe, and younger brother Dominic chose careers in baseball. The three of them became major league All-Stars and scored more runs than any brotherly combination in history!

On the recommendation of brother Vince, Joe was signed to play shortstop for the Seals at the age of 17. He was shifted to the outfield in his second season when he set a minor-league record by hitting safely in 61 consecutive games. It was a sign of things to come. In 1935, Joe helped San Francisco to a Pacific Coast League Championship and was named the league's Most Valuable Player (MVP). He was already under contract with the Yankees where he made his highly publicized New York debut the following spring.

Joltin' Joe DiMaggio took Major League Baseball by storm. He set AL rookie records for triples and runs scored, and his 22 outfield assists led the league. Between 1936 and 1941 he won two AL batting championships and his first home run crown, while the Yankees won the World Championship in all but one season. Joe was named the

league's MVP in 1939 and again in 1941, the season in which his 56 game hitting streak set the all-time Major League Baseball record!

After 31 months of voluntary duty in the United States Air Force, Joe returned for six more seasons as the Yankees' centerfielder. He won a third AL MVP Award in 1947, and a second home run crown the following season. In 1947, New York ended a three year pennant drought and won the World Championship in four of the next five seasons. The "Yankee Clipper" retired after the team's victory in the 1951 Fall Classic. That season Joe DiMaggio shared the Yankee Stadium outfield with a rookie by the name of Mickey Mantle.

PROFILE:
Joe DiMaggio
Born: November 25, 1914
Height: 6' 2"
Weight: 193 pounds
Position: Outfield
Teams: New York Yankees (1936-1942, 1946-1951)

9

CHAMPIONSHIP

SEASONS

1936
World Series
New York Yankees (4) vs.
New York Giants (2)

1937
World Series
New York Yankees (4) vs.
New York Giants (1)

1938
World Series
New York Yankees (4) vs.
Chicago Cubs (0)

1939
World Series
New York Yankees (4) vs.
Cincinnati Reds (0)

1941
World Series
New York Yankees (4) vs.
Brooklyn Dodgers (1)

1947
World Series
New York Yankees (4) vs.
Brooklyn Dodgers (3)

1949
World Series
New York Yankees (4) vs.
Brooklyn Dodgers (1)

1950
World Series
New York Yankees (4) vs.
Philadelphia Phillies (0)

1951
World Series
New York Yankees (4) vs.
New York Giants (2)

THE STREAK

Joe DiMaggio's 56 game hitting streak in 1941 is among the most enduring records in baseball history. The incredible feat began on May 15, gained national attention when he unofficially extended it in the All-Star Game, and finally ended on July 17. It broke the previous mark set by 'Wee' Willie Keeler, who "hit 'em where they ain't" in 44 straight games back in 1897. Unlike Keeler, Joe was a power-hitter and went deep 30 times during the season of "The Streak." Amazingly, Joltin' Joe struck-out only 13 times that season. It took a pair of defensive gems from the Cleveland Indians third baseman Ken Keltner to bring Joe's marathon to the finish line. He started a 16 game hitting streak the next day!

Joe DiMaggio

GOOD-BYE NORMA JEANE

Joe DiMaggio was among the most popular people in America for several years. In 1939, he married a moviestar and nightclub singer named Dorothy Arnold. The marriage lasted five years, after which Joe began taking to the Hollywood and New York City night life. When his baseball career was over, he married world famous pinup girl and Hollywood actress, Marilyn Monroe. Their marriage was even shorter than Joe's first, but the couple remained friends for the rest of Monroe's life. For decades after her death, fresh flowers appeared at her grave each day. Many speculate that they came from DiMaggio.

Joe swats one out.

ALL IN THE FAMILY

Joe, Dominic, and Vince DiMaggio combined to form one of Major League Baseball's most productive families. Together they accounted for nearly 5,000 hits, and all three were outstanding defensive outfielders.

In 1941, Dom and Joe made the first-ever brotherly appearance in an All-Star Game. "The Little Professor" headed to rightfield as a late-inning substitute to play alongside Joe in center. In the eighth inning, Joe doubled and Dom singled him home. In the 1949 All-Star Game, Joe drove in Dom with what proved to be the margin of victory.

Vince made his two All-Star appearances while brothers Joe and Dominic were serving in the military during World War II. In one of those contests, Vince went three-for-three, including a ninth inning home run!

Mickey Mantle

In the 1950s, Major League Base-ball in New York City reached its peak. In a decade when American teenagers were "rockin' 'round the clock" with Bill Haley's Comets, the capital of baseball was rolling to 14 pennants and 8 World Champion-ships! The New York Yankees, Brooklyn Dodgers, and New York Giants formed a powerful triumvi-rate, each with its own baseball palace and resident legend in centerfield.

The Polo Grounds was home to Willie Mays, Ebbets Field had Duke Snider, and Yankee Stadium housed the great Mickey Mantle. Inter-city arguments abounded over which borough's batsman was best. The "Bronx Bombers" took 4 of 5 "Subway Classics" in the 1950s, and the Giants and Dodgers headed to California before the decade was up. Mean-while, the "Big Apple's" baseball tradition was car-ried into the 1960s by the New York Yankees and their "Commerce Comet." Willie, Mickey, and "the Duke" were

all eventually enshrined into the Baseball Hall of Fame.

Mickey Charles Mantle was born in Spavinaw, Oklahoma. He was brought up to be a baseball player. His father Elvin named his oldest son after the legendary catcher Gordon "Mickey" Cochrane. Elvin was a right-handed pitcher in a semiprofessional league, before retiring to the zinc and lead mines of northern Oklahoma. "I always wished my dad could be somebody else than a miner," Mickey said. "I knew it was killing him. He was underground eight hours a day. Every time he took a breath, the dust and dampness went into his lungs."

Mutt Mantle, as Mickey's father was more commonly known, did every-thing he could to ensure his son would not receive a similar fortune to his own. Mutt's father Charles Mantle was a left-hander who had pitched for the mining company's baseball team. Together, Mutt and Charlie began teaching Mickey to be a switch-hitter at the age of five. He practiced from the left side of the plate against his father's pitch-ing and from the right side against Grandpa.

Mickey's extended-family had moved to Commerce, Oklahoma, when he was four years old. At Commerce High School, he played basketball, football, and baseball, earning his nickname "The Com-merce Comet." While playing in a summer league, an umpire sug-gested he ask for a tryout with the Yankee farm club in Joplin, Missouri.

Mickey said later, "I walked into the Joplin ball park one day in May, 1949, and asked the manager to give me a chance. Three weeks later, a week after I graduated from high school, the Yankees signed me."

Mickey Mantle moved into the "House that Ruth Built" in 1951. The next season, he took over Joe DiMaggio's vacated spot in centerfield. In 18 major league seasons, the Mick participated in 12 Fall Classics. His 18 World Series homers surpassed a record for-merly held by the Babe himself. Like Babe Ruth, many of Mickey's 536 career home runs were knocked clear out of the yard. His blast off the Yankee Stadium rightfield facade was estimated at 602 feet, and is often credited as the longest home run in baseball history!

PROFILE:
Mickey Mantle
Born: November 20, 1931
Died: August 13, 1995
Height: 5' 11"
Weight: 198 pounds
Position: Outfield
Teams: New York Yankees (1951-1968)

CHAMPIONSHIP

SEASONS

1951

World Series
New York Yankees (4) vs.
New York Giants (2)

1952

World Series
New York Yankees (4) vs.
Brooklyn Dodgers (3)

1953

World Series
New York Yankees (4) vs.
Brooklyn Dodgers (2)

1956

World Series
New York Yankees (4) vs.
Brooklyn Dodgers (3)

1958

World Series
New York Yankees (4) vs.
Milwaukee Braves (3)

1961

World Series
New York Yankees (4) vs.
Cincinnati Reds (1)

1962

World Series
New York Yankees (4) vs.
San Francisco Giants (3)

M&M BOYS

Mickey Mantle was one of many star players to play for the Yankees in the 1950s. Joe DiMaggio, Yogi Berra (C), Johnny Mize (1B), and Whitey Ford (P), were all teammates of the Mick who were elected to the Hall of Fame.

In 1960, Mickey Mantle was joined in the Yankee's outfield by Roger Maris. Mickey won the last of his four home run crowns that season, out-homering Maris by only one (40-39). The next season, the "M & M Boys" put on a two-man power display that has never been matched.

Both players were in pursuit of Babe Ruth's 34 year old record of 60 home runs in a single-season. A mysterious virus caused the Mick to miss eight games during the stretch drive, and he finished with a career-high of 54 homers. Roger Maris broke the Babe's record hitting his 61st homer on the final day of the 1961 season.

Mantle hitting left handed.

TAPE MEASURE SHOTS

On April 17, 1953, Mickey Mantle hit a long home run that cleared the leftfield bleachers at Washington's Griffith Stadium. The mammoth blast landed in a neighboring yard, where an interested bystander got out a tape-measure to determine its distance from home plate. The 565 foot drive is credited with inventing the term "tape-measure shot," and is considered among the longest homers in the history of the game.

The length of a batted ball can be determined by calculating its height and distance at its peak trajectory. One of Mickey's two shots off the distant Yankee Stadium facade came just inches from leaving the yard. It was still rising!

Mickey Mantle

S WITCH

Mickey Mantle hit 373 homers left handed and another 163 from the right side of the plate. He was also one of the fastest runners in the game despite numerous knee surgeries and other career threatening ailments. He won the AL MVP Award in 1956, 1957, and 1962. In 1956, he led the league with a .353 batting average, 52 home runs, and 130 RBIs, joining Lou Gehrig as the only Yankees to achieve a Triple Crown season! His manager Casey Stengel called Mickey "the best one-legged player I ever saw." The Mick was quite simply the greatest switch-hitter who ever played the game.

Mantle hitting right handed.

Willie Mays

Enthusiasm is a measure of the passion a person brings with them into their daily lives. It can be contagious and inspire groups of people toward tremendous accomplishments. When Willie Mays became a member of the New York Giants in 1951, he infected the team and its fans with his love for baseball. Seemingly out of the pennant-chase, the team won 37 of their final 44 games to catch the Brooklyn Dodgers on the last day of the season. The Giants became National League Champions when Bobby Thompson's game-winning homer ended a three game playoff. Willie was named the NL's Rookie of the Year and thus began the career of the incredibly enthusiastic "Say Hey Kid!"

Willie Howard Mays was born in Fairfield, Alabama. He was the only child of Ann and William Mays, who were divorced during his early childhood. Willie's father was a professional baseball player for the Birmingham Barons of the Negro National League, and later worked as a plumber's assistant. Willie's mother was remarried and had 10 more children with her second husband. Sarah Mays, Willie's beloved aunt, raised him after his parents were separated.

Baseball was part of Willie's life from the very beginning. At the age of three, he began playing catch with his father. As a 14 year old, he was good enough to play for the local steel mills and semiprofessional teams. Fairfield Industrial High School did not have a baseball team, but Willie played football and basketball. Before graduating, his father persuaded the manager of the Barons to give his son a tryout. Willie became a professional baseball player at the age of 17. During the school year, he played only on

Sundays and in the Birmingham area. When summer vacation arrived, he joined the everyday lineup in centerfield.

Willie was renowned for his defensive ability as well as for his powerful bat. When a pair of the Giants' scouts came to Birmingham to observe the team's first baseman, they found an unexpected fortune in centerfield. One of them called New York and reportedly stated, "That first baseman won't do, but I saw a young kid of an outfielder that I can't believe . . . You've got to get this boy." Willie signed a contract and was sent to the Giants' minor league system for development. In his second season, he was clubbing opposing pitchers to the tune of a .477 batting average when he received the call to come to the big leagues.

After his tremendous rookie season, Willie's career was interrupted by the Korean War. His service in the United States Army lasted two years and in the end cost him a shot at Babe Ruth's all-time home run mark. When he returned, he began a string of 20 consecutive All-Star seasons. In

1954, Willie Mays was the NL's batting champion and MVP. In Game 1 of that season's World Series, he chased a long drive off the bat of Vic Wertz to the deepest regions of New York's Polo Grounds. The play, known in baseball lore as "The Catch," robbed the Cleveland Indians of a scoring opportunity and set the stage for the Giants' last World Championship in New York.

As a San Francisco Giant, Willie became the NL's MVP for a second time in 1965. He won his fourth home run crown that season, and the next year he surpassed Mel Ott for the league's all-time long-ball leadership. He ended his career as a member of the New York Mets, where his last hit produced a game-winning RBI in the 1973 World Series. The Say Hey Kid never lost his enthusiasm for the game he loved.

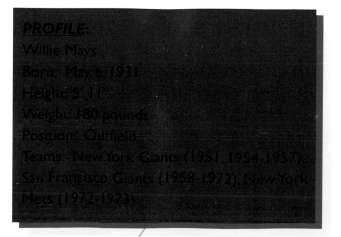

PROFILE:
Willie Mays
Born: May 6, 1931
Height: 5' 11"
Weight: 180 pounds
Position: Outfield
Teams: New York Giants (1951, 1954-1957),
San Francisco Giants (1958-1972), New York
Mets (1972-1973)

17

CHAMPIONSHIP
SEASONS

Mays makes a round trip after hitting one out of the park

1954

World Series
New York Giants (4) vs.
Cleveland Indians (0)

THE VERY BEST?

When Willie Mays first arrived in the major leagues he struggled at the plate. Frustrated by his lack of offensive production he begged manager Leo Durocher to send him back to the minor leagues. Durocher, whose own playing career began in 1925, comforted his young rookie by saying, "You're my centerfielder as long as I'm the manager because you're the best centerfielder I've ever seen." The next game Mays homered off Warren Spahn, the first of 660 round-trippers he would smack during his career. Spahn later said, "I'll never forgive myself. We might have gotten rid of Willie forever if I'd only struck him out."

STICKBALL

Willie was a popular hero in New York City. Early in his career he lived in Harlem, where he regularly could be found playing stickball in the streets with neighborhood children. His characteristic greeting "Say Hey" became a lasting nickname and popular song. "I like to play happy," he would say. "Baseball is a fun game, and I love it."

Willie Mays takes a huge cut at the ball.

GOLDEN LEATHER

The Gold Glove Award was established in 1957 to acknowledge each league's finest defensive players. That season, Willie Mays was the lone selection as the NL's Gold Glove outfielder. Since then, each league has selected three players, representing the three outfield positions. Willie was among the three NL Gold Glove outfielders in 12 straight seasons!

Willie Mays hits one into deep center.

GODFATHER

In 1956, Willie Mays became the first player in major league history to collect 30 home runs and 30 stolen bases in one season. He accomplished the feat three times in his career, and later became the first to reach the 300 HR/300 SB plateau in a career. The next player to reach such standards was Willie's San Francisco Giant teammate Bobby Bonds.

When Bobby Bonds had a son named Barry, Willie became the child's Godfather. In 1996, Barry Bonds joined his father and Godfather in the 300/300 club.

19

Henry
Aaron

Horse racing is known as the "Sport of Kings" for its long tradition dating back to ancient Greece. Baseball, while it is not nearly as old, has royalty all of its own. When Babe Ruth surpassed Roger Connor's previous all-time home run mark (138) in 1921, he was officially crowned as Major League Baseball's Home Run King. Babe held the title for more than 50 years and was not alive to witness the coronation of his successor. That man was "Hammerin' Hank" Aaron, whose reign continues to this day.

Henry Louis Aaron was born in Mobile, Alabama. He was one of Herbert and Estella Aaron's five children. Hank's father was a boilermaker's helper at a local shipyard. The family lived in an ordinary house in a section of town known as Toulminville. As a boy, Hank liked to pass his time by hitting bottle-caps with a broomstick. He would later credit the habit for helping to develop his lightning-fast swing. "A bottle cap will swerve at the last instant," he said. "You've got to go out and get it."

Hank was 13 years old when Jackie Robinson broke baseball's long-standing policy of racial segregation. The so-called Gentleman's Agreement among major league owners had lasted more than 60 seasons, during which time some of the greatest players of all-time toiled in the various Negro Leagues. It was in one such league where baseball's future Home Run King would begin his own professional career.

The Indianapolis Clowns were a barnstorming Negro League organization akin to basketball's Harlem Globetrotters. They signed Hank to play

shortstop after an exhibition game with his hometown team, the Mobile Black Bears, in the spring of 1952. Hank began traveling with the Clowns immediately earning a salary of $200 a month. He never did understand why they claimed to hail from Indianapolis. "We never made it to Indiana the whole time I was with the team."

It wasn't long before Hank began to make an impression on major league scouts. He was refused a tryout with the Brooklyn Dodgers, who felt the 18 year old was too skinny to hit for power. After receiving a tip from Clowns' owner Syd Pollock, the Milwaukee Braves gave Hank the opportunity he was looking for. They sent him to their minor league affiliate in Eau Claire, Wisconsin, where Hank completed the 1952 season and was voted the Northern League's Rookie of the Year.

Henry Aaron made his major league debut on April 13, 1954. The next season, he began a streak of 21 straight All-Star appearances. In 1957, Hank was named the National League's Most Valuable Player (MVP) after collecting the first of

his four single-season home run crowns, and hitting a pennant-clinching shot in a late September game against the Cardinals. In the 1957 World Series, Hank led all hitters in runs, hits, homers, batting average, and RBIs, as the city of Milwaukee celebrated their only World Championship.

The Braves moved to Atlanta, Georgia, in 1966, where Hammerin' Hank continued his torrid home run pace through nine more seasons. His 40 homers in 1973, left him one shy of the immortal Babe Ruth's 714. The next season, Hank tied the race in his first at-bat. Four nights later, on April 8, 1974, Henry Aaron was crowned baseball's new Home Run King!

PROFILE:
Henry Aaron
Born: February 5, 1934
Height: 6'
Weight: 180 pounds
Position: Outfield
Teams: Milwaukee Braves (1954-1965), Atlanta Braves (1966-1974), Milwaukee Brewers (1975-1976)

*Hank Aaron hitting
for the Braves.*

1957
World Series
Milwaukee Braves (4) vs.
New York Yankees (3)

ROYAL FLUSH

Just as Babe Ruth had done before him, Hank Aaron ended his professional career in the city where it began. He was traded from the Atlanta Braves to the Milwaukee Brewers where he played two seasons and hit the last of his 755 home runs. Hank is also baseball's all-time leader in RBIs (2,297), extra-base hits (1,477), and total bases (6,856).

Hank Aaron smashes a homer.

SILENCE IS GOLDEN

Henry Aaron typically went about his business with quiet consistency. He was neither a flashy performer nor one who easily accepted praise. "My arrival in the major leagues was pretty dull. No drama, no excitement, absolutely none. I just arrived, that's all," he remembers.

On top of being the most productive offensive player in baseball history, Hank was also outstanding on defense. Before his rookie season, he was converted from a shortstop to an outfielder while playing winter ball in Puerto Rico. In the 14 World Series games that he was involved in, Hank played without an error. He was named the National League's Gold Glove rightfielder three times.

Hammerin' Hank broke Babe's "unbreakable record."

HOSEN ONE

At the age of 34, Hank had hit 481 homers. Like many players in that stage of their careers, he began to ponder his retirement. Rather than hanging up his spikes, he renewed himself with a mission of greatness. "I believed, and I still do, that there was a reason why I was chosen to break the record. It's my task to carry on where Jackie Robinson left off," he said.

Many people were taken by surprise when Hank suddenly began to approach Babe's "unbreakable record." "I was tired of being invisible. I was the equal of any ballplayer in the world, and if nobody was going to give me my due, it was time to grab for it," he recalls. At the age of 39, Hammerin' Hank cracked 40 homers for the eighth time in his career. The next season he completed his mission, launching number 715 in front of a national television audience!

Frank
Robinson

Jackie Robinson integrated Major League Baseball in 1947, opening the way for all people to have the opportunity of competing on the same playing field. Jackie became the first player to receive baseball's Rookie of the Year honor that season, and two years later was named the NL's MVP. After nearly 100 years of existence, the professional Negro Leagues had all but faded out of sight by the end of the 1950s. Meanwhile, Willie Mays, Henry Aaron, Roy Campenella, Don Newcombe, and Ernie Banks accounted for eight more MVP Awards won by African Americans in their first full decade of major league play.

Frank Robinson was the NL's Rookie of the Year in 1956. He won the league's MVP Award in 1961, after guiding the Cincinnati Reds to the NL Pennant. Frank was traded to the Baltimore Orioles in 1966, where he completed a Triple Crown season and led the team to its first World Championship. He was named the AL's MVP that season, making him the only player to win the award in both leagues. Frank launched a total of 586 homers in his career, placing him fourth on the all-time list behind Henry Aaron, Babe Ruth, and Willie Mays.

The youngest of Ruth Shaw's 10 children, Frank Robinson was born in Beaumont, Texas. His mother and father were separated during his infancy. When Frank was four years old, Ruth moved with her children to Oakland, California. In their west-side neighborhood, Frank became a regular on the playgrounds and in motion-picture theaters. Delivering newspapers earned him money for the movies, while he earned his reputation on the local ball fields.

Frank excelled in all of the sports he participated in, but baseball became his passion. "Football and basketball," he said "for me were things to do while waiting for the baseball season." Frank made the All-City Basketball Team as a senior at McClymonds High School. Among his teammates that season was the legendary Bill Russell (see *Champion NBA Big Men).* Russell went on to the University of San Francisco and later won 11 NBA Championships with the Boston Celtics. Frank was signed by the Cincinnati Reds when he graduated from high school.

As a minor-league baseball player, Frank encountered racial discrimination for the first time. It began in the Pioneer League, where in his team's home town of Ogden, Utah, the theaters were "For Whites Only." The following two seasons he played in the Southern League, where facing racial epithets became an everyday experience. While their efforts on the field were finally being recognized, African American players were still being forced to room in separate hotels from their white teammates in many cities.

Just as Jackie Robinson had done before him, Frank Robinson rose above the fear and anger to become one of Major League Baseball's all-time greatest players. After winning a second World Championship in Baltimore, Frank's career took a variety of turns. In 1975, he became the Cleveland Indians' player-manager. It was another ground-breaking step for African Americans and the major leagues. Frank and Jackie Robinson are not related, but were similar in name, race, and stature as pioneers of Major League Baseball.

PROFILE:
Frank Robinson
Born: August 31, 1935
Height: 6' 1"
Weight: 195 pounds
Position: Outfield
Teams: Cincinnati Reds (1956-1965), Baltimore Orioles (1966-1971), Los Angeles Dodgers (1972), California Angels (1973-1974), Cleveland Indians (1974-1976)

CHAMPIONSHIP

SEASONS

Frank Robinson

1966
World Series
Baltimore Orioles (4) vs.
Los Angeles Dodgers (0)

1970
World Series
Baltimore Orioles (4) vs.
Cincinnati Reds (1)

RED-FACED

Cincinnati's trade of Frank Robinson ranks with Boston's sale of Babe Ruth among baseball's all-time blunders. After six All-Star appearances in ten seasons, the Reds' management labeled Frank an "over-the-hill malcontent" and shipped him off to Balti-more. Cincinnati dropped to seventh place in the NL that season, while Frank led the American League in nearly every offensive category. Frank played six seasons in Baltimore, carrying the Orioles to four AL pennants and two World Championships! He was an AL All-Star five times including one appearance as a California Angel.

Frank Robinson stands up to the plate.

JACKIE'S LAST REQUEST

Jackie Robinson integrated the Baseball Hall of Fame in 1962, and became a strong symbol for the Civil Rights Movement in that decade. In the final years of his life, he made repeated pleas for baseball and the world to eliminate discrimination. "I'd like to live to see a Black manager," he stated before a live television audience at the 1972 World Series. Jackie died nine days later, his wishes unfulfilled.

On Opening Day 1975, Frank Robinson became the first African American to manage in the major leagues. He also hit a home run that helped the Indians gain the victory. In 1981, Frank took over as manager for the San Francisco Giants breaking the NL's "color-line" for that position. The next season, he joined Jackie Robinson in the Baseball Hall of Fame.

Jackie Robinson preceded Frank in overcoming discrimination in baseball.

A LEAGUE OF HIS OWN

Frank Robinson is in a class by himself as a two league player. He's the only man to be chosen MVP in both leagues, to hit All-Star Game homers for both, and to hit 200 or more home runs in both the American and National Leagues. In 1989, Frank was named AL's Manager of the Year for his job in guiding the Baltimore Orioles. It matched the NL honor he had won seven years earlier while managing the San Francisco Giants.

Roberto Clemente

Dedication is what causes a person to focus and commit themselves toward their goals. When an individual achieves greatness in pursuit of a goal, they become honored for that commitment. Roberto Clemente balanced his dedication to the game of baseball with an obligation towards people in need. "If you have an opportunity to make things better and you don't, then you are wasting your time on this earth," he would say.

Roberto Walker Clemente was born in Carolina, Puerto Rico. He was raised on a sugarcane plantation, where his parents performed various responsibilities. "My mother and father, they worked like racehorses for me," he remembers. Occasionally young Roberto would sneak away to peek through an outfield fence where he saw future major leaguers playing winter-baseball. His favorites were a pair of Negro League outfielders named Monte Irvin and Willie Mays.

It was on a softball diamond, where young Roberto's own talents first became apparent. At the age of 17, he was spotted by the owner of a local hard-ball team called the Santurce Cangrejeros. They played their games in a professional winter league, where Roberto once shared the outfield with his hero the "Say Hey Kid." Roberto played three seasons with the Cangrejeros, and eventually came to the attention of a Brooklyn Dodgers' scout. He signed a minor-league contract and was sent to the team's International League team in Montreal, Quebec.

Roberto's one season with the Dodger organization would be the most difficult of his career. A rule at the time made him eligible to be drafted by any team willing to offer a major league contract. No one explained this to Roberto, and while the Dodgers didn't offer him a big league contract of their own, they attempted to hide his talent in Canada. "If I struck out I stayed in the lineup. If I played well I was benched," Roberto said later. "One day I hit three triples and was benched the next day."

Hurt and confused, Roberto returned to Puerto Rico after the season where things soon made a turn for the worse. His brother was dying of a brain tumor, and on the way to visit him, Roberto's car was plowed into by a drunk-driver. The back injuries he suffered from the accident would aggravate him throughout his career. They did not prevent Roberto Clemente from becoming one of the greatest baseball players in the history of the game.

The Pittsburgh Pirates were not fooled by Brooklyn's "secret." Roberto became the Pirates' rightfielder the next season (1955). The team finished in last place that season, but five years later they became World Champions. In 1961, Roberto won the first of his 12 straight Gold Glove Awards, a streak that tied him with Willie Mays as the most by an outfielder. He also won the first of four NL batting crowns that season. In

1966, he was named the league's MVP, after hitting a career-high 29 home runs.

Roberto's finest performance came in the 1971 World Series. He was named MVP of the seven game battle while helping the Pirates to another World Championship. After 18 seasons in the major leagues, Roberto Clemente cracked his 3,000 hit on September 30, 1972. Later that year while leading a relief effort to aid victims of a Nicaraguan earthquake, the plane he was traveling on crashed into the ocean. Roberto's fabulous baseball career was recognized with his immediate induction into the Baseball Hall of Fame. His supreme sacrifice was venerated with the Hall's introduction of the Roberto Clemente Award. The annual honor is dedicated in memory of his commitment to good citizenship.

PROFILE:
Roberto Clemente
Born: August 18, 1934
Died: December 31, 1972
Height: 5' 11"
Weight: 175 pounds
Position: Outfield
Teams: Pittsburgh Pirates (1955-1972)

CHAMPIONSHIP
SEASONS

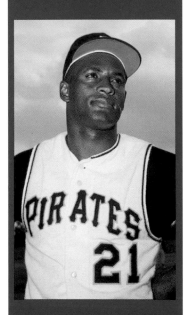

Roberto Clemente

1960
World Series
Pittsburgh Pirates (4) vs.
New York Yankees (3)

1971
World Series
Pittsburgh Pirates (4) vs.
Baltimore Orioles (3)

CITIZENSHIP

One of Roberto Clemente's many commitments to citizenship was to oversee the construction of a large sports complex for kids. Roberto felt getting kids involved in sports would keep them off the streets.

Roberto was wildly popular in his native land. In 1970, Pittsburgh's brand new Three River Stadium hosted "Roberto Clemente Day" in his honor. He received a scroll containing 300,000 Puerto Rican signatures representing 10 percent of the island's population. Roberto later declined a serious offer to run for Mayor of his hometown, fearing his election would be based on his athletic notoriety.

Clemente up to bat.

TRAGEDY

When Roberto learned that relief shipments he had organized to aid Nicaraguan earthquake victims were being mishandled, he decided to take matters into his own hands. While most of Puerto Rico was celebrating New Year's Eve and preparing for the inauguration ceremony of their new governor, Roberto was boarding an overloaded cargo plane he had personally rented bound for the devastated Central American country. The plane crashed shortly after takeoff killing all of its passengers. The new governor's inaugural festivities were canceled, as every member of the Pittsburgh Pirates flew to Puerto Rico for the funeral of baseball's greatest citizen.

Roberto Clemente with the Pirates.

WHY WAIT?

The Baseball Hall of Fame waived its five year waiting period between retirement and eligibility in the case of Roberto Clemente, electing him in 1973. The only other player to receive such gratitude was Lou Gehrig, whose career with the New York Yankees was ended by a deadly disease. Roberto became the first Latin American player inducted into baseball's sanctuary. Coincidentally, he entered the "Hall" with his childhood hero Monte Irvin.

Reggie Jackson

Performance in clutch situations is what determines a player's value to their team. A rally-stopping defensive play or a key hit can mean the difference between winning and losing. When that play comes in the World Series, it often separates the *Champions* from the also-rans. Reggie Jackson's Fall Classic performances earned him the nickname "Mr. October." He was a member of five World Championship teams in his career with the Oakland Athletics and New York Yankees. Other players have won more titles, but Reggie remains the only person who has been named the World Series' Most Valuable Player more than once.

Reginald Martinez Jackson was one of six children born to Mr. and Mrs. Martinez Jackson. His parents were divorced early in his life, and Reggie moved with his father to Cheltenham, Pennsylvania, near Philadelphia. Martinez Jackson was a professional baseball player for the Newark Eagles of the Negro National League in the late 1920s and early 1930s. Later in life, he supported his family with a small tailoring and dry cleaning business.

From the time of his childhood, Reggie's greatest accomplishments came through athletics. At Cheltenham High School he was a varsity performer in football, basketball, baseball, and track. He pitched three no-hitters and batted over .500 in his senior baseball season, but was even more acclaimed as a star halfback for the football team. After graduating, Reggie accepted a scholarship from Arizona State University to play on the gridiron.

Reggie played safety for the Sun Devil's football team as a freshman. When the season ended he accepted a five dollar wager to try out for the university's powerful baseball squad. He made an immediate impression on Coach Bobby Winkles, earned a spot on the roster, and won the bet! As a sophomore, Reggie played centerfield and led the team in runs, hits, and RBIs. He was named to the college All-America team, and was chosen by the Kansas City Athletics in Major League Baseball's 1966 amateur draft.

After a season and a half in the minor leagues, Reggie made his Kansas City debut in 1967. The next season he became the starting centerfielder in the team's new home of Oakland, California. He nearly eclipsed the record for strikeouts in a season that year, after whiffing 171 times! In his second full-season he was on pace to break the single-season home run (61) mark, before slumping in September to finish with 47. "I couldn't handle all that pressure," he said. "Everyday somebody was coming up to me and asking if I could pass Ruth and Maris. It really got to me."

After a disappointing 1970 season, Reggie traveled to Puerto Rico to play winter ball with the Santurce Cangrejeros. There he met his hero and manager-in-training, Frank Robinson. "He was trying to do too much," Frank advised. "He had to be told he can't carry a whole club." Frank and Reggie paced the AL to an All-Star victory the next season, and faced off in the 1971 American League Championship Series. Frank's Orioles defeated the A's and advanced to the World Series. The next season, Reggie's Athletics began a three year string of World Championships.

Reggie Jackson's most memorable performance came in the 1977 World Series. After homering in Game 4 and Game 5, he connected three straight times in Game 6 to bring the New York Yankees their first World Championship without Mantle, DiMaggio, or Ruth. Reggie was the MVP of the series, just as he had been with the 1973 Oakland Athletics. Mr. October had once again lived-up to his name in the Fall Classic.

PROFILE:
Reggie Jackson
Born: May 18, 1946
Height: 6' 1"
Weight: 180 pounds
Position: Outfield
Teams: Kansas City Athletics (1967), Oakland Athletics (1968-1975, 1987), Baltimore Orioles (1976), New York Yankees (1977-1981), California Angels (1982-1986)

CHAMPIONSHIP

SEASONS

1972
World Series
Oakland Athletics (4) vs.
Cincinnati Reds (3)

1973
World Series
Oakland Athletics (4) vs.
New York Mets (3)

1974
World Series
Oakland Athletics (4) vs.
Los Angeles Dodgers (1)

1977
World Series
New York Yankees (4) vs.
Los Angeles Dodgers (2)

1978
World Series
New York Yankees (4) vs.
Los Angeles Dodgers (2)

MR. OCTOBER

Reggie Jackson missed the 1972 World Series after tearing a muscle in his leg while stealing home in the final game of that season's American League Championship Series. In 1973, he was the AL's MVP after winning his first of four home run crowns. He carried his hot hitting into the Fall Classic where he led the team with six RBIs and made two spectacular catches in Game 7 to earn the Series' MVP Award as well.

Reggie homered in the opener of the 1974 Series, doubled in Game 2, and threw out a key baserunner in Game 5, as the Athletics won the World Championship for the third-straight time.

Reggie was dubbed Mr. October for his post-season performance.

CANDY FROM A BABY

When Reggie Jackson was signed by the New York Yankees, he predicted there would be a candy bar named after him. He had a tendency to boast, leading one former teammate to comment, "There isn't enough mustard in the whole world to cover that hot dog."

In the tradition of the "Oh-Henry" named for Hank Aaron, the "Reg-gie" bar was in fact introduced after his record-setting performance in the 1977 World Series. Contrary to popular belief, the "Baby Ruth," was not named for the famous Yankee slugger. That candy bar had already been named in honor of President Grover Cleveland's young daughter, Ruth.

Reggie, taking his usual huge cut.

*F*ALL CLASSIC

Reggie's five homers in the 1977 Fall Classic set a single-series record. Four of those long balls came in consecutive official at bats! After driving one out in his final at bat of Game 5, he was walked in his first appearance of Game 6. In his next three trips to the plate, Reggie hit home runs off the first pitch of three separate Dodger hurlers. Babe Ruth is the only other player to accomplish a home run trifecta in a World Series game. The Bambino did it twice!

Kirby Puckett

Mix the enthusiasm of Willie Mays with the right-handed hitting prowess of Joe DiMaggio. Add Babe Ruth's popularity and an irreplaceable smile. Pack it all into a five-foot, eight-inch frame of solid muscle. These are the ingredients necessary to create the lumpy, little, lovable, legend, named Kirby Puckett. Few, if any, have ever hit a baseball harder, chased one farther, or thrown with more pinpoint accuracy than this good natured hero of the Minnesota Twins.

Hilarious and humble, Kirby was the most popular player of his day. The "human-cube" helped bring a pair of World Championships to the Twin Cities. When an irreversible case of glaucoma caused him to retire at the age of 35, the collective baseball world shed a tear. "Just because I can't see, doesn't mean God doesn't answer prayers," he said to a room-full of grown men who sobbed uncontrollably. "Tomorrow is not promised to any of us, so enjoy yourself."

Kirby Puckett was born in a south-side ghetto of Chicago, Illinois. His father was a postal worker, and

Kirby's mother was a housewife with 10 children. The family lived in a 14th floor apartment, where the elevator rarely functioned and violence surrounded them. "I had five older brothers who took care of me," Kirby remembers. "I would come home from school, do my homework, then look for kids to play ball with. If nobody would play, I would just throw strikes against the wall or hit rolled-up socks in my room."

At Calumet High School, Kirby was among the top of his class academically and a star third baseman for the baseball team. It was there where he began the rigorous weight-training schedule that would eventually form his block-like figure. "Not too many scouts would come to watch baseball teams play in the ghetto," he said. When no colleges or universities offered Kirby a scholarship, he went to work full-time for the Ford Motor Company, but was laid-off in a matter of months.

The apparent misfortune of losing his job at the factory inspired Kirby to redouble his efforts toward a career in baseball. He attended a Kansas City Royals tryout camp, where he was noticed by coach Dewey Kalmer of Bradley University. Kalmer offered Kirby a baseball scholarship and moved him to centerfield. In one season at Bradley, Kirby was named to the Missouri Valley All-Conference team. When the season ended, he received notice that his father had died. "I wanted to quit school and take care of my mom," he said. "I called her and told her I was coming home. She told me 'No, no, you're going to make it big. You're going to be good one day.'"

Despite his mother's encouragement, Kirby transferred closer to home where he enrolled at Triton Community College. There, he led the baseball team to the Junior College National Finals, and was discovered by Jim Rantz, a minor-league scout for the Minnesota Twins. "He stood out," Rantz said.

"It wasn't because he had a home run, a double, stole two bases, threw a guy out at home and had a shaved head either. The enthusiasm he had on a miserably hot night, when everybody was dog tired ... that was the thing you noticed!"

After two outstanding seasons in the Twins' minor-league system, Kirby was called-up to the big leagues. In his major league debut he cracked four hits and never looked back. In 12 seasons, Kirby led the AL in hits four times. His .356 batting average in 1988, was the highest by a right-handed batter since Joe DiMaggio hit .357 in 1941. The next season, he won the league's batting crown. Kirby won six Gold Glove Awards in centerfield and was an All-Star 10 times. His absence from the 1996 Mid-Summer Classic caused annual AL All-Stars like Cal Ripken, Jr. and Ken Griffey, Jr. to comment "It's just not the same without Puck.'"

PROFILE:
Kirby Puckett
Born: March 14, 1961
Height: 5' 8"
Weight: 210 pounds
Position: Outfield
Teams: Minnesota Twins (1984-1995)

CHAMPIONSHIP
SEASONS

Kirby Puckett rounding the bases after hitting a World Series home run.

1987
World Series
Minnesota Twins (4) vs.
St. Louis Cardinals (3)

1991
World Series
Minnesota Twins (4) vs.
Atlanta Braves (3)

ENJOY YOURSELF

Kirby always had a knack for making difficult situations a little easier to handle. As a boy growing up in a gang-infested Chicago neighborhood he did not allow any bad influences to disrupt him from having a good time. "I was always out playing," he recalls. "My brothers saw to it that nobody messed with me. To me, a real good time was getting up early in the summertime and going out and playing baseball all day. It was not really that important, the gangs and all that stuff. I was a kid enjoying myself."

In 1992, Kirby was elected to his seventh-straight All-Star Game. Ken Griffey, Jr. was voted in for the third straight time that season. When Griffey wondered aloud which of the two would start in centerfield, he presented an interesting dilemma for the AL's manager, Tom Kelly. In typical fashion, Kirby diffused the situation with humor. "You take center," Kirby told Griffey during the workout day. "You're younger than me. You still like to run. Remember, anything in the gap is yours!"

Kirby blasts a shot into leftfield.

JUST HACKIN'

Kirby Puckett was a notorious 'bad-ball' hitter. "I just go up there hackin'," he would say. Kirby began his major league career as a lead-off hitter who regularly bunted his way on base. In his first two seasons he hit a total of only four home runs. After moving to the third spot in the batting order after some instruction from another Twins' legend, Tony Oliva, Kirby hacked a career high 31 homers in his third season. In 1989, Puck joined Oliva and Ty Cobb as the only AL players to lead the league in hits for three straight seasons.

Kirby, just hackin' away.

ULTIPLES

Kirby Puckett's hits often came in bunches. He had 65 multiple-hit games in 1987, including six games with four hits or more. Kirby also had a habit of combining his multi-hit games with defensive gems. In one contest with the Milwaukee Brewers, he tied an AL record with six hits and robbed Robin Yount of a grand-slam with a brilliant, over-the-fence, leaping grab! Combined with the four hits he collected the previous night, Kirby's ten consecutive hits had also tied a major league record.

Perhaps his most memorable multi-hit performance came in Game 6 of the 1991 World Series. Once again, he started the evening with a leaping, back-to-the-wall catch, this time robbing Ron Gant of an extra-base hit. Kirby then proceeded to go 3-for-4 with a single, triple, and game-winning, 11th inning home run!

David
Justice

Justice is a quality of fairness. It is to uphold what is right. In an American court of law, the judge and jury determine what is just. On the baseball diamond, justice is upheld by the umpire. When there is a close call, the umpire's opinion is the only one that matters. Players and managers must go along with what the umpire says, or eventually they will be asked to leave the premises.

Major League Baseball also has David Justice. He was the NL's 1990 Rookie of the Year, and since then has appeared in the World Series four times as a member of the Atlanta Braves. His home run in Game 6 of the 1995 World Series gave Atlanta their only World Championship.

David Christopher Justice was born in Cincinnati, Ohio. He is the only child of Nettie and Robert Justice. When David was four years old, his father left the family. Nettie went to work as a housekeeper and earned extra money catering dinner parties. "It was always a

sacrifice, because I didn't think of myself, I just thought of David," she remembers. "We always had plenty of food, I had a coat to keep warm, and a roof over our heads."

At the age of 12, David entered Covington Latin School in Covington, Kentucky, just across the Ohio River from his home in Cincinnati. "The school was not for the weak," he says of the academically enriched program that requires students to skip the seventh and eighth grades. "Everyone was smart. As a 13 year old sophomore you take Latin, German, chemistry, computer science, biology, history, and English. The homework is unbelievable!" As a 15 year old senior, David made the Catholic All-America high school basketball team. He also played football and baseball, but because of his relative youth, college athletic scholarships were hard to come by.

College recruiters told David if he stayed in high school two more years, he could be one of the greatest basketball prospects in state history. The idea seemed silly since he was about to graduate, so he accepted a basketball scholarship from Thomas More College, a small school in Crestview Hills, Kentucky. David hated the three mile runs his new basketball coach required for training. One day he drifted off-course and headed for the baseball field. He made a successful tryout, and within two years the coach was saying "David Justice is the greatest baseball player I've ever seen!"

The Atlanta Braves drafted David after his junior season. He spent the better part of five years in the minor leagues, before moving to

Atlanta in 1990. Since then, David's career has been a mixture of great success and disappointment. The World Series glory of 1995 has been tempered with three Fall Classic failures, a season-ending baseball strike, and a number of disabling injuries.

Before the 1997 season, David Justice was traded to the Cleveland Indians in a deal that sent Kenny Lofton to Atlanta. Injuries caused a love-hate relationship between Braves' fans and their former star outfielder, which he felt was unjust. Through it all, David has proven himself to be a *Champion*. Will he go down in history among baseball's all-time greats? The jury is still out.

PROFILE:
David Justice
Born: April 14, 1966
Height: 6' 3"
Weight: 195 pounds
Position: Outfield
Teams: Atlanta Braves (1989-1996), Cleveland Indians (1997-)

CHAMPIONSHIP

SEASONS

David Justice blasts one.

1995

World Series
Atlanta Braves (4) vs. Cleveland Indians (2)

MISTRIAL

David Justice has the potential to be one of Major League Baseball's all-time great *Sluggers*. After his Rookie of the Year season in 1990, he has suffered through a series of mishaps. When a sore back forced him out of the Braves' lineup in 1991, broadcasters, fans, and teammates questioned the extent of the injury. "First of all, I was leading the league in RBIs when I got hurt. I was on my way to having a pretty good season, and we still had two weeks left in the first half," David said. "Why would I want to sit out? That makes absolutely no sense." It was later discovered that he had indeed suffered a stress-fracture of his lower vertebrae.

David's best statistical season came in 1993. Many attributed the turnaround to his new wife, movie star Halle Berry. David and Halle became media darlings as both were named to *People Magazine's* list of the 50 Most Beautiful People in the World. Like DiMaggio and Monroe, their marriage was short-lived.

Justice slides into home plate.

CHOP THIS

Atlanta Braves' fans waited 20 seasons for their first World Championship. When the team made its first appearance in the Fall Classic in 1991, Fulton County Stadium became known as the "Chop Shop," for the enthusiastic crowd and their signature chant the "Tomahawk Chop." After two World Series failures, the team felt a sense of urgency to get the job done in 1995. The Cleveland Indians defeated the Braves in Game 5, and the Atlanta fans began to sense their fortunes slipping away for a third time.

Justice tags a line-drive.

Angered by the crowd's reaction after the loss, David Justice spoke out. "You have to do something great to get them out of their seats," he said. "If we don't win, they'll probably burn our houses down!" The next morning, newspaper headlines reported "JUSTICE TAKES A RIP AT BRAVES FANS."

Afterward, David would admit the comments caused him tremendous stress. "It was the most pressure I've ever felt in my life. My head hurt, my stomach hurt, and all I could think about was going out on the field and getting booed by 50,000 fans." When he was introduced before Game 6, the Atlanta fans gave him the cold reception he was expecting.

The game itself remained tied through five innings, before David's solo-blast provided the only scoring. With their first World Championship secured, the "Chop Shop" released their anxiety in a shower of appreciation. David made his own amends with the Atlanta faithful by saying, "The fans proved me wrong. They were gems tonight!"

Glossary

All-American: A person chosen as the best amateur athlete at their position.

All-Star: A player who is voted by fans as the best player at his position in a given year. American and National League All-Stars have been facing off each summer since 1933 in the All-Star Game.

American League Championship Series (ALCS): A best of seven game playoff with the winner going to the World Series to face the National League Champions.

Batting Average: A baseball statistic calculated by dividing a batters hits by the number of times at bat.

Contract: A written agreement a player signs when they are hired by a professional team.

Defense: The part of a team attempting to prevent the opposition from scoring.

Draft: A system in which new players are distributed to professional sports teams.

Earned Run Average (ERA): A baseball statistic that calculates the average number of runs a pitcher gives up per nine innings of work.

Freshman: A student in the first year of a U.S. high school or college.

Hall of Fame: A memorial for the greatest players of all time located in Cooperstown, New York.

Home Run (HR): A play in baseball where a batter hits the ball over the outfield fence scoring everyone on base as well as themselves.

Junior: A student in the third year of a U.S. high school or college.

Major Leagues: The highest ranking associations of professional baseball teams in the world, currently consisting of the American and National Baseball Leagues.

Minor leagues: A system of professional baseball leagues at levels below Major League Baseball.

National League (NL): An association of baseball teams formed in 1876 that make up one half of the major leagues.

National League Championship Series (NLCS): A best of seven game playoff with the winner going to the World Series to face the American League Champions.

Pennant: A flag that symbolizes the championship of a professional baseball league.

Pitcher: The player on a baseball team who throws the ball for the batter to hit. He stands on a mound and pitches the ball toward the strike zone area above the plate.

Plate: The place on a baseball field where a player stands to bat. It is used to determine the width of the strike zone. It is also the final goal a baserunner must reach to score a run.

Professional: A person who is paid for their work.

RBI: A baseball statistic standing for *runs batted in*. A player receives an RBI for each run that scores on their hit.

Rookie: A first-year player, especially in a professional sport.

Senior: A student in the fourth year of a U.S. high school or college.

Sophomore: A student in the second year of a U.S. high school or college.

Stolen Base (SB): A play in baseball when a baserunner advances to the next base while the pitcher is delivering his pitch.

Strikeout: A play in baseball when a batter is called out for failing to put the ball in play after the pitcher has delivered three strikes.

Triple Crown: A rare accomplishment when a single player finishes a season leading their league in batting average, home runs, and RBIs. A pitcher can win a Triple Crown by leading his league in wins, ERA, and strikeouts.

Varsity: The principal team representing a university, college, or school in sports, games, or other competitions.

Veteran: A player with more than one year of professional experience.

Walk: A play in baseball when a batter receives four pitches out of the strike zone and is allowed to go to first base,

World Series: The championship of Major League Baseball played since 1903 between the pennant winners from the American and National leagues.

Index